ROALD DAHL'S

EXTRAORDINARY FRIENDS

working in
partnership
with

ILLUSTRATED BY QUENTIN BLAKE

PUFFIN

PUFFIN BOOKS

UK | USA | Canada | Ireland | Australia
India | New Zealand | South Africa

Puffin Books is part of the Penguin Random House group of companies
whose addresses can be found at global.penguinrandomhouse.com.

puffinbooks.com

Penguin
Random House
UK

Made for McDonald's 2015
001

The BFG: first published in Great Britain by Jonathan Cape Ltd 1982
The Giraffe and the Pelly and Me: first published in Great Britain by Jonathan Cape 1985
Published in paperback by Puffin Books

Printed in Slovakia

A CIP catalogue record for this book is available from the British Library

ISBN: 978–0–141–36252–6

The National Literacy Trust is a registered charity no. 1116260 and a company limited
by guarantee no. 5836486 registered in England and Wales and a registered charity in
Scotland no. SC042944. Registered address: 68 South Lambeth Road, London SW8 1RL.
National Literacy Trust logo and reading tips copyright © National Literacy Trust, 2014

www.literacytrust.org.uk/donate

Batch nr.: 123912/16

FSC
MIX
FSC® C022120

Explore the extraordinary world of

ROALD DAHL

Find out what happens when Sophie is taken
all the way to Giant Country by her new friend,
the Big Friendly Giant. The BFG is
no ordinary giant. He **won't** gobble
you up. Oh no – he's very kind. And he
has a **special** way with words.

Or perhaps you'd like an even more **UNUSUAL
FRIEND**? A giraffe? A pelican? Maybe a monkey!

Bring Roald Dahl's extraordinary stories
to life with the **Happy Studio** app.
Simply download the app to a phone
or tablet and read the stories in this
book aloud to experience the fun.

The Marvellous Ears

from

THE BFG

In the cave, the Big Friendly Giant sat Sophie down on the enormous table. 'Is you quite snuggly there?' he asked. 'You isn't fridgy cold?'

'I'm fine,' Sophie said.

'I cannot help thinking,' said the BFG, 'about your poor mother and father. By now they must be jipping and skumping all over the house shouting "Hello hello where is Sophie gone?"'

'I don't have a mother and father,' Sophie said. 'They both died when I was a baby.'

'Oh, you poor little scrumplet!' cried the BFG. 'Is you not missing them very badly?'

'Not really,' Sophie said, 'because I never knew them.'

'You is making me sad,' the BFG said, rubbing his eyes.

'Don't be sad,' Sophie said. 'No one is going to be worrying too much about me. That place you took me from was the village orphanage. We are all orphans in there.'

'You is a norphan?'

'Yes.'

'How many is there in there?'

'Ten of us,' Sophie said. 'All little girls.'

'Was you happy there?' the BFG asked.

'I hated it,' Sophie said.

'The woman who ran it was called Mrs Clonkers and if she caught you breaking any of the rules, like getting out of bed at night or not folding up your clothes, you got punished.'

'How is you getting punished?'

'She locked us in the dark cellar for a day and a night without anything to eat or drink.'

'The rotten old rotrasper!' cried the BFG.

'It was horrid,' Sophie said. 'We used to dread it. There were rats down there.

We could hear them creeping about.'

'The filthy old fizzwiggler!' shouted the BFG. 'That is the horridest thing I is hearing for years! You is making me sadder than ever!' All at once, a huge tear that would have filled a bucket rolled down one of the BFG's cheeks and fell with a splash on the floor. It made quite a puddle.

Sophie watched with astonishment. 'What a strange and moody creature this is,' she thought. 'One moment he is telling me my head is full of squashed flies and the next moment his heart is melting for me because Mrs Clonkers locks us in the cellar.'

'The thing that worries *me*,' Sophie said, 'is having to stay in this dreadful place for the rest of my life. The orphanage was pretty awful, but I wouldn't have been there for ever, would I?'

'All is my fault,' the BFG said. 'I is the one who kidsnatched you.' Yet another enormous tear welled from his eye and splashed on to the floor.

'Now I come to think of it, I won't actually be here all that long,' Sophie said.

'I is afraid you will,' the BFG said.

'No, I won't,' Sophie said. 'Those giant brutes out there are bound to catch me sooner or later and have me for tea.'

'I is *never* letting that happen,' the BFG said.

For a few moments the cave was silent. Then Sophie said, 'May I ask you a question?'

The BFG wiped the tears from his eyes with the back of his hand and gave Sophie a long thoughtful stare. 'Shoot away,' he said.

'Would you please tell me what you were doing in our village last night? Why were you poking that long trumpet thing into the Goochey children's bedroom and then blowing through it?'

'Ah-ha!' cried the BFG, sitting up suddenly in his chair. 'Now we is getting nosier than a parker!'

'And the suitcase you were carrying,' Sophie said. 'What on earth was *that* all about?'

The BFG stared suspiciously at the small girl sitting cross-legged on the table.

'You is asking me to tell you whoppsy big secrets,' he said. 'Secrets that nobody is ever hearing before.'

'I won't tell a soul,' Sophie said. 'I swear it. How could I anyway? I am stuck here for the rest of my life.'

'You could be telling the other giants.'

'No, I couldn't,' Sophie said. 'You told me they would eat me up the moment they saw me.'

'And so they would,' said the BFG. 'You is a human bean and human beans is like strawbunkles and cream to those giants.'

'If they are going to eat me the moment they see me, then I wouldn't have time to tell them anything, would I?' Sophie said.

'You wouldn't,' said the BFG.

'Then why did you say I might?'

'Because I is brimful of buzzburgers,' the BFG said. 'If you listen to everything I am saying you will be getting earache.'

'Please tell me what you were doing in our village,' Sophie said. 'I promise you can trust me.'

'Would you teach me how to make an elefunt?' the BFG asked.

'What *do* you mean?' Sophie said.

'I would dearly love to have an elefunt to ride on,' the BFG said dreamily. 'I would so much love to have a jumbly big elefunt and go riding through green forests picking peachy fruits off the trees all day long. This is a sizzling-hot muckfrumping country we is living in. Nothing grows in it except snozzcumbers. I would love to go somewhere else and pick peachy fruits in the early morning from the back of an elefunt.'

Sophie was quite moved by this curious statement.

'Perhaps one day we will get you an elephant,' she said. 'And peachy fruits as well. Now tell me what you were doing in our village.'

'If you is really wanting to know what I am doing in your village,' the BFG said, 'I is blowing a dream into the bedroom of those children.'

'*Blowing a dream?*' Sophie said. 'What *do* you mean?'

'I is a dream-blowing giant,' the BFG said. 'When all the other giants is galloping off every what way and which to swollop human beans, I is scuddling away to other places to blow dreams into the bedrooms of sleeping children. Nice dreams. Lovely golden dreams. Dreams that is giving the dreamers a happy time.'

'Now hang on a minute,' Sophie said. 'Where do you get these dreams?'

'I collect them,' the BFG said, waving an arm towards all the rows and rows of bottles on the shelves. 'I has billions of them.'

'You can't *collect* a dream,' Sophie said. 'A dream isn't something you can catch hold of.'

'You is never going to understand about it,' the BFG said. 'That is why I is not wishing to tell you.'

'Oh, please tell me!' Sophie said. 'I *will* understand! Go on! Tell me how you collect dreams! Tell me everything!'

The BFG settled himself comfortably in his chair and crossed his legs. 'Dreams,' he said, 'is very mysterious things. They is floating around in the air like little wispy-misty bubbles. And all the time they is searching for sleeping people.'

'Can you see them?' Sophie asked.

'Never at first.'

'Then how do you catch them if you can't see them?' Sophie asked.

'Ah-ha,' said the BFG. 'Now we is getting on to the dark and dusky secrets.'

'I won't tell a soul.'

'I is trusting you,' the BFG said. He closed his eyes and sat quite still for a moment, while Sophie waited.

'A dream,' he said, 'as it goes whiffling through the night air, is making a tiny little buzzing-humming noise. But this little buzzy-hum is so silvery soft, it is impossible for a human bean to be hearing it.'

'Can *you* hear it?' Sophie asked.

The BFG pointed up at his enormous truck-wheel ears which he now began to move in and out. He performed this exercise proudly, with a little proud smile on his face. 'Is you seeing these?' he asked.

'How could I miss them?' Sophie said.

'They maybe is looking a bit propsposterous to you,' the

We look **better** in colour!

BFG said, 'but you must believe me when I say they is very extra-usual ears indeed. They is not to be coughed at.'

'I'm quite sure they're not,' Sophie said.

'They is allowing me to hear absolutely every single twiddly little thing.'

'You mean you can hear things I can't hear?' Sophie said.

'You is *deaf as a dumpling* compared with me!' cried the BFG. 'You is hearing only thumping loud noises with those little earwigs of yours. But I am hearing *all the secret whisperings of the world*!'

'Such as what?' Sophie asked.

'In your country,' he said, 'I is hearing the footsteps of a ladybird as she goes walking across a leaf.'

'*Honestly?*' Sophie said, beginning to be impressed.

'What's more, I is hearing those footsteps *very loud*,' the BFG said. 'When a ladybird is walking across a leaf, I is hearing her feet going *clumpety-clumpety-clump* like giants' footsteps.'

'Good gracious me!' Sophie said. 'What else can you hear?'

'I is hearing the little ants chittering to each other as they scuddle around in the soil.'

'You mean you can hear ants talking?'

'Every single word,' the BFG said. 'Although I is not exactly understanding their langwitch.'

'Go on,' Sophie said.

'Sometimes, on a very clear night,' the BFG said, 'and if I is swiggling my ears in the right direction' – and here he swivelled his great ears upwards so they were facing the ceiling – 'if I is swiggling them like this and the night is very clear, I is sometimes hearing faraway music coming from the stars in the sky.'

A queer little shiver passed through Sophie's body. She sat very quiet, waiting for more.

'My ears is what told me you was watching me out of your window last night,' the BFG said.

'But I didn't make a sound,' Sophie said.

'I was hearing your heart beating across the road,' the BFG said. 'Loud as a drum.'

'Go on,' Sophie said. 'Please.'

'I can hear plants and trees.'

'Do *they* talk?' Sophie asked.

'They is not exactly talking,' the BFG said. 'But they is making 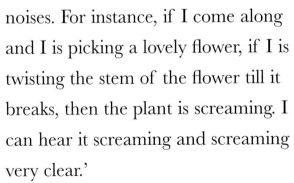 noises. For instance, if I come along and I is picking a lovely flower, if I is twisting the stem of the flower till it breaks, then the plant is screaming. I can hear it screaming and screaming very clear.'

'You don't mean it!' Sophie cried. 'How awful!'

'It is screaming just like you would be screaming if someone was twisting *your* arm right off.'

'Is that really true?' Sophie asked.

'You think I is swizzfiggling you?'

'It is rather hard to believe.'

'Then I is stopping right here,' said the BFG sharply. 'I is not wishing to be called a fibster.'

'Oh no! I'm not calling you anything!' Sophie cried. 'I believe you! I do really! Please go on!'

The BFG gave her a long hard stare. Sophie looked right back at him, her face open to his. 'I believe you,' she said softly.

She had offended him, she could see that.

'I wouldn't ever be fibbling to you,' he said.

'I know you wouldn't,' Sophie said. 'But you must understand that it isn't easy to believe such amazing things straight away.'

'I understand that,' the BFG said.

'So do please forgive me and go on,' she said.

He waited a while longer, and then he said, 'It is the same with trees as it is with flowers. If I is chopping an axe into the trunk of a big tree, I is hearing a terrible sound coming from inside the heart of the tree.'

'What sort of sound?' Sophie asked.

'A soft moaning sound,' the BFG

said. 'It is like the sound an old man is making when he is dying slowly.'

He paused. The cave was very silent.

'Trees is living and growing just like you and me,' he said. 'They is alive. So is plants.'

He was sitting very straight in his chair now, his hands clasped tightly together in front of him. His face was bright, his eyes round and bright as two stars.

'Such wonderful and terrible sounds I is hearing!' he said. 'Some of them you would never wish to be hearing yourself! But some is like glorious music!'

When the BFG speaks to his friend Sophie, he gets **squiff-squiddled** and creates **extraordinary** new words.

Can you match each of the BFG's special **Gobblefunk** words with its meaning in English?

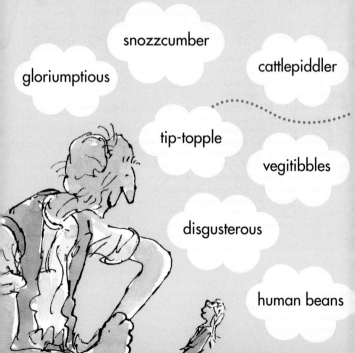

snozzcumber

gloriumptious

cattlepiddler

tip-topple

vegitibbles

disgusterous

human beans

Sophie has matched one word to help you.

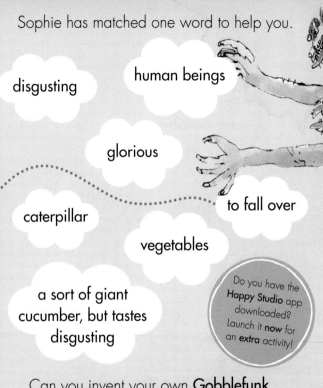

disgusting

human beings

glorious

to fall over

caterpillar

vegetables

a sort of giant
cucumber, but tastes
disgusting

Do you have the **Happy Studio** app downloaded? Launch it **now** for an **extra** activity!

Can you invent your own **Gobblefunk**
word here to mean **extraordinary**?

• •

disgusterous = disgusting   gloriumptious = glorious
vegibbles = vegetables   human beans = human beings   catflepiddler = caterpillar
snozzcumber = disgusting cucumber

Meet Billy and
his Friends

from

THE GIRAFFE AND
THE PELLY AND ME

Not far from where I live there is a queer old empty wooden house standing all by itself on the side of the road. I long to explore inside it but the door is always locked, and when I peer through a window all I can see is darkness and dust. I know the ground floor used once to be a shop because I can still read the faded lettering across the front which says THE GRUBBER. My mother has told me that in our part of the country in the olden days a grubber was another name for a sweet-shop, and now every time I look at it I think to myself what a lovely old sweet-shop it must have been.

On the shop-window itself somebody has painted in white the words FOR SAIL.

One morning, I noticed that FOR SAIL had been scraped off the shop-window and in its place somebody had painted SOLED. I stood there staring at the new writing and wishing like mad that it had been me who had bought

it because then I would have been able
to make it into a grubber all over again.
I have always longed and longed to
own a sweet-shop. The sweet-shop of
my dreams would be loaded from top
to bottom with Sherbet Suckers and
Caramel Fudge and Russian Toffee and
Sugar Snorters and Butter Gumballs
and thousands and thousands of other
glorious things like that. Oh boy, what
I couldn't have
done with
that old

Grubber shop if it had been mine!

On my next visit to The Grubber, I was standing across the road gazing at the wonderful old building when suddenly an enormous bathtub came sailing out through one of the second-floor windows and crashed right on to the middle of the road!

A few moments later, a white porcelain lavatory pan with the wooden seat still on it came flying out of the same window and landed with a wonderful splintering crash just beside the bathtub. This was followed by a kitchen sink and an empty canary-cage and a four-poster bed and two hot-water bottles and a rocking horse and a sewing-machine and goodness knows what else besides.

It looked as though

some madman was ripping out the whole of the inside of the house, because now pieces of staircase and bits of the banisters and a whole lot of old floorboards came whistling through the windows.

Then there was silence. I waited and waited but not another sound came from within the building. I crossed the road and stood right under the windows and called out, 'Is anybody at home?' There was no answer.

In the end it began to get dark so

I had to turn away and start walking home. But you can bet your life nothing was going to stop me from hurrying back there again tomorrow morning to see what the next surprise was going to be.

When I got back to The Grubber house the next morning, the first thing I noticed was the new door. The dirty old brown door had been taken out and in its place someone had fitted a brand-new red one. The new door was fantastic. It was twice as high as the other one had been and it looked ridiculous. I couldn't begin to imagine who would want a tremendous tall door like that in his house unless it was a giant.

As well as this, somebody had scraped away the SOLED notice on the shop-window and

THE LADDERLESS
WINDOW-CLEANING
COMPANY~

Get your windows
cleaned without
a lot of dirty
ladders leaning
against your
house

now there was a whole lot of different writing all over the glass. I stood there reading it and reading it and trying to figure out what on earth it all meant.

I tried to catch some sign or sound of movement inside the house but there was none . . . until all of a sudden . . . out of the corner of my eye . . . I noticed that one of the windows on the top floor was slowly beginning to open outwards . . .

Then a HEAD appeared at the open window. I stared at the head. The head

stared back at me with
big round dark eyes.

Suddenly, a second
window was flung wide
open and of all the crazy
things a gigantic white bird hopped
out and perched on the window-sill. I
knew what this one was because of its
amazing beak, which was shaped like
a huge orange-coloured
basin. The Pelican
looked down at me and
sang out:

'Oh, how I wish
For a big fat fish!
I'm as hungry as ever could be!
A dish of fish is my only wish!
How far are we from the sea?'

'We are a long way from the sea,'
I called back to him, 'but there is a
fishmonger in the village not far away.'

'A fish *what*?'

'A fish*monger*.'

'Now what on earth would that be?'
asked the Pelican. 'I have heard of a
fish-*pie* and a fish-*cake* and a fish-*finger*,

but I have never heard of a fish-*monger*. Are these mongers good to eat?'

This question baffled me a bit, so I said, 'Who is your friend in the next window?'

'She is the Giraffe!' the Pelican answered. 'Is she not wonderful? Her legs are on the ground floor and her head is looking out of the top window!'

As if all this wasn't enough, the window on the *first floor* was now flung wide open and out popped a Monkey!

The Monkey stood on the window-sill and did a jiggly little dance. He was so skinny he seemed to be made only out of furry bits of wire, but he danced wonderfully well, and I clapped and cheered and did a little dance myself in return.

'We are the Window-Cleaners!' sang out the Monkey.

THE LADDERLESS
WINDOW-CLEANING
COMPANY

Get your windows
cleaned without
a lot of dirty
ladders leaning
against your
house.

'We will polish your glass
Till it's shining like brass
And it sparkles like sun on the sea!
We are quick and polite,
We will come day or night,
The Giraffe and the Pelly and me!

We're a fabulous crew,
We know just what to do,
And we never stop work to drink tea.
All your windows will glow
When we give them a go,
The Giraffe and the Pelly and me!

We use water and soap
Plus some kindness and hope,
But we never use ladders, not we.
Who needs ladders at all
When you're thirty feet tall?
Not Giraffe, and not Pelly! Not me!'

I stood there enthralled. Then I heard the Giraffe saying to the Pelican in the next window, 'Pelly, my dear, be so good as to fly down and bring that small person up here to talk to us.'

At once the Pelican spread his huge white wings and flew down on to the

road beside me. 'Hop in,' he said,
opening his enormous beak.

I stared at the great orange beak
and backed away.

'Go ON!' the Monkey shouted from
up in his window. 'The Pelly isn't going
to *swallow* you! Climb IN!'

I said to the Pelican, 'I'll only get in

if you promise not to shut your beak
once I'm inside.'

'You have nothing to fear!' cried the
Pelican,

And let me tell you why.

I have a very special beak!

A special beak have I!

You'll never see a beak so fine,

I don't care where you go.

There's magic in this beak of mine!

Hop in and don't say NO!'

'I will *not* hop in,' I said, 'unless you
swear on your honour you won't shut it

once I'm inside. I don't like small dark places.'

'When I have done what I am just about to do,' said the Pelican, 'I won't be *able* to shut it. You don't seem to understand how my beak works.'

'Show me,' I said.

'Watch this!' cried the Pelican.

I watched in amazement as the top half of the Pelican's beak began to slide smoothly backwards

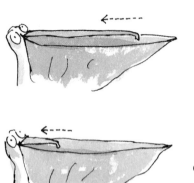

into his
head until
the whole
thing was
almost out
of sight.

'It bends

and goes down

inside the back of my neck!' cried the

Pelican. 'Is that not sensible? Is it not

magical?'

'It's unbelievable,' I said. 'It's exactly

like one of those metal tape-measures

my father's got at home. When it's out, it's straight. When you slide it back in, it bends and disappears.'

'Precisely,' said the Pelican. 'You see, the top half is of no use to me unless I am chewing fish. The bottom half is what counts, my lad! The bottom half of this glorious beak of mine is the bucket in which we carry our window-cleaning water! So if I didn't slide the top half away I'd be standing around all day long holding it open!

'So I slide it away
For the rest of the day!
Even so, I'm still able to speak!
And wherever I've flown
It has always been known
As the Pelican's Patented Beak!

If I want to eat fish
(That's my favourite dish)
All I do is I give it a tweak!
In the blink of an eye
Out it pops! And they cry,
"It's the Pelican's Patented Beak!" '

'*We are the Window-Cleaners!*'
sang out the Monkey.

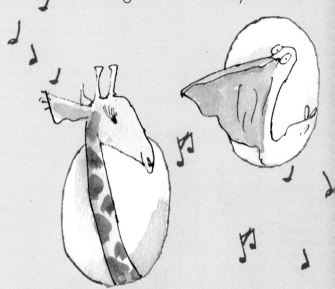

'We will **polish** your **glass**
Till it's **shining** like **brass**
And it sparkles like **sun on the sea**!'

The Monkey is a fine singer and **songwriter**. Can you **replace** the **bold** words with your own to turn this into an **extraordinary** new song for you and your friends to sing?

Do you have the **Happy Studio** app downloaded? Launch it **now** for an **extra** activity!

Fun with these EXTRAORDINARY FRIENDS doesn't end here!

The **Happy Studio** app has extra activities linked to this book. Download it now to a phone or tablet.

And you can delve deeper into the extraordinary world of

ROALD DAHL

at **www.roalddahl.com**